THE LITTLE SNOWPLOW

LORA KOEHLER illustrated by JAKE PARKER

SCHOLASTIC INC.

On the Mighty Mountain Road Crew, the trucks came in one size: **BIG.**

That is, until a new snowplow joined the crew.

"You're such a little snowplow," the big trucks said.
"Leave the heavy lifting to us."
And off they roared.

So all spring, the little snowplow cleared streams
while the big trucks bulldozed mudslides.

In the summer, he cleaned up after parades
while the big trucks built roads.

In the fall, he pushed leaves into piles
while the big trucks mounded mountains of salt and sand.

As fall turned into winter,
the little snowplow began training.
He made the light on top go around
and blew his horn:

Beep, beep!

He drove forward and back.
Then he raised and lowered
his plow. Ten times. Fast!

Everything was in working order. He could hardly wait for snow.

"Ha!" said the dump truck. "You've never even seen snow!"

The little snowplow ignored him.
He knew what snow was.

"Why, I remember snow up to the eaves,"
said a cement mixer.

"Yeah, we had a big,
strong snowplow then,"
the garbage truck said.

"Too bad she retired,"
the utility truck said.
"I heard she moved to
a beach in Florida."

"I hope it doesn't snow like that this winter,"
the dump truck said.
"It might be too much for a little snowplow.
We'd probably have to help."

The little snowplow turned his bumper on the trucks.

But that night, he raised and lowered his plow ten extra times.

And the next day,
he added even more exercises.
He pushed loads of gravel.
He pulled blocks of concrete.
Just in case.

One morning, Will, the road-crew foreman, burst in before dawn.
"It's a real blizzard out there!"

The dump truck snorted.
"Looks like there's already more than
a little snowplow can handle."

Beep, beep, VROOOM!

The drifts looked soft and fun to the little snowplow.

"Let's go!" Will said.
They drove out into the storm.

The little snowplow cleared the streets of Mighty Mountain. But it kept snowing.

So the little snowplow cleared the streets of Mighty Mountain again.
It snowed harder, and the wind began to howl.

Once more, the little snowplow started to clear the streets.
Deep drifts swirled around his treads.
Icy gusts blew against his windshield.

Snow piled up higher than he could raise his plow.
He wondered if he should have done more plow lifts.

"This one's too big for anyone to handle on their own," Will said.
He called for backup.

"I knew that plow would need help,"
the dump truck grumbled as he drove out.

The little snowplow wiped his windshield and kept plowing.
Silver Fork, Stampede Avenue, Main Street. That's when he heard a rumbling.
He saw the dump truck drive by. Then the little snowplow heard a thundering.
He turned the corner of Main and Ridge . . .

. . . just as an avalanche swept down the mountain.

WHOOSH!

BEEP, BEEP, BEEEEP!

the little snowplow cried.

“He’s buried!” Will yelled. “No time to lose!
But it will take hours
for the big trucks to move that boulder.”

The little snowplow drove forward.
He backed up. He repositioned.
He edged forward and squeezed past the boulder.

“Way to go, half-pint,” Will said.
“The big trucks couldn’t have gotten through.”

CINEMA

The little snowplow plunged his plow into the avalanche debris.

He dug

and dug

and dug.

His engine shuddered. His exhaust sputtered.

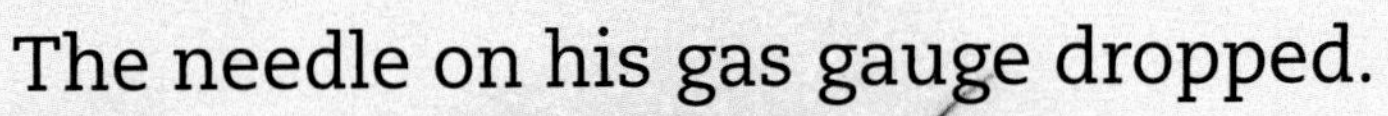

The needle on his gas gauge dropped.

Will pointed. "There he is!"
The little snowplow
dug faster.

Creeeeak! Crack!

More snow crashed behind him.
"Hurry!" Will said.
Shovels of snow flew in all directions.

Will raced to attach a cable between the trucks.
The little snowplow drove forward, tugging.
The dump truck revved his engine. His wheels spun.

The little snowplow braced himself and **PULLED**. Just as he had practiced.
The dump truck's wheels gained traction.
The little snowplow gave a mighty **TUG** . . .

and
pulled the
dump truck free!

"Wooo-hoooo!"

Will cheered.

The dump truck shook snow from his truck bed.
"I didn't know a snowplow so little could be so strong!" he said.

Beep, beep! The little snowplow blew his horn.
Together, the two trucks worked to clear the boulder.

When they finally got back to the garage, all the other trucks

honked and beeped and blinked. "Great job!" they shouted.

The little snowplow's headlights sagged.
His plow dragged. His gas tank was nearly empty.
But before turning in for the night,
he made the light on top go around.
He blew his horn:

Beep . . . beep.

He drove forward. And back.
Then he raised and lowered his plow.
Ten times. Slow.

Everything was in working order. He could hardly wait for sleep.

For my mom and dad, who taught me to think "I can."

L. K.

For Dad, who taught me the importance of hard work.

J. P.

ISBN 978-1-338-14445-1

Published by Scholastic Inc., 557 Broadway, New York, NY 10012, by arrangement with Candlewick Press.

12 11 10 9 8 7 6 5 4 3 2 16 17 18 19 20 21

Printed in the U.S.A. 08

First Scholastic printing, December 2016

This book was typeset in PMN Caecilia.
The illustrations were done in pencil and rendered digitally.